822.60

GUARD DOG

by Philip Wooderson
illustrated by David Burroughs
Cover illustrated by Nathan Lueth

DANGER
KEEP OUT

Librarian Reviewer
Katharine Kan
Graphic novel reviewer and Library Consultant, Panama City, FL
MLS in Library and Information Studies, University of Hawaii at Manoa, HI

Reading Consultant
Elizabeth Stedem
Educator/Consultant, Colorado Springs, CO
MA in Elementary Education, University of Denver, CO

STONE ARCH BOOKS
Minneapolis   San Diego

First published in the United States in 2008
by Stone Arch Books
151 Good Counsel Drive, P.O. Box 669
Mankato, Minnesota 56002
www.stonearchbooks.com

Originally published in Great Britain in 1999
by A & C Black Publishers Ltd
38 Soho Square, London, W1D 3HB

Library of Congress Cataloging-in-Publication Data
Wooderson, Philip.
  Guard Dog / by Philip Wooderson; illustrated by David Burroughs.
  p. cm. — (Graphic Quest)
  Originally published: London: A. & C. Black, 1999.
  ISBN-13: 978-1-59889-829-3 (library binding)
  ISBN-10: 1-59889-829-9 (library binding)
  ISBN-13: 978-1-59889-885-9 (paperback)
  ISBN-10: 1-59889-885-X (paperback)
  1. Graphic novels. I. Burroughs, Dave, 1952– II. Title.
PN6727.W66G87 2008
741.5'973—dc22   2007006244

Summary: Ryan would rather play video games than help his dad sell artwork at
the flea market. When the artwork is stolen, however, Ryan and his friend take on
the case. The two boys quickly learn that a detective's work is no game.

Art Director: Heather Kindseth
Graphic Designer: Brann Garvey

1 2 3 4 5 6 12 11 10 09 08 07

Printed in the United States of America

TABLE OF CONTENTS

JUV
W886g

CHAPTER ONE

I didn't want to go to the flea market, but Dad saw this as his chance to stop me from playing *Guard Dog* the rest of Saturday morning.

You play that game so much, you're starting to **look** like a guard dog.

GUARD DOG

BLEEP BLEEP BLEEP

So I went with Dad to see about renting a booth for him to sell his woodwork. Dad got the last one. He was happy until the market man told him he had to pay the rent up front.

Pay all of it now?

If you don't like it, you don't have to have a booth.

I could see Dad was getting ready to start an argument. I gave him a jab with my elbow.

Come on, Dad, just pay up.

Dad slapped down the money, and we left.

Outside, a man who had been in line
ahead of us caught up with Dad.

Dad had been working hard every evening for weeks turning
out lamp stands, salad bowls, spoons, and doorstops.

9

CHAPTER TWO

Dad woke me up at 5:30 the next morning.

Uh, what?

Time to get up, Ryan.

We were out of the house before the sun came up. But our car wasn't there.

It's been stolen!

Dad quickly called the police.

My woodworking supplies have been stolen as well! I'll lose my first day of trading and the rent on the booth.

Could we have the car's license number? Then we can put out a search, sir.

The rest of the morning went by slowly. Dad thumbed through papers, and I bleeped away on my video game, trying to dodge the Guard Dog. Top score 190.

That noise is driving me crazy!

BLEEP BLEEP BLEEP

Can I call Steve and ask him to come over?

CHAPTER THREE

We found the car on a grimy street by the railroad tracks. The thief had smashed the window and hot-wired the ignition. There was already a parking ticket on the windshield.

Then we cruised around town for an hour. Dad stopped to search every alley, but we didn't find any of his woodworking supplies. Not even a single lamp stand!

As soon as we got home, Dad called the market office to tell them why we weren't there.

After the phone call, Dad left me in peace. He went off to the lumberyard to buy himself some more wood. When he came home, he shut himself in the work shed and got busy. Dad didn't ask me to help. After a couple of hours bleeping away at *Guard Dog* (best score 203), I was bored out of my mind.

I decided to head over to Steve's house.

18

19

Steve picked up a video of *Death Dungeon 2*.

You're too young!

Yeah? Better than being too old.

We browsed around the rest of the market. Most of the booths were boring, except for one selling old comics. As we were walking toward it, Steve tugged my arm.

Look, Ryan.

Wally and Den's Wooden Objects.

Ob-jets.

You sound just like your Dad.

Thanks.

Wally spotted us and called us over.

Your dad chickened out?

I would have told him about the car and supplies being stolen, but I noticed what Wally was wrapping.

Hey, Steve, I recognize that!

It looks like one of Dad's lamp stands!

24

25

I looked back at Wally's booth. A man in a black leather jacket was there now. Wally handed him a fat envelope. As the man walked away, I saw the back of his jacket.

We followed, keeping our distance. We watched him far ahead of us as he turned onto Main Street. For a moment I thought we lost him. When I spotted him again, he was climbing into a big black pick-up truck parked with two tires on the curb.

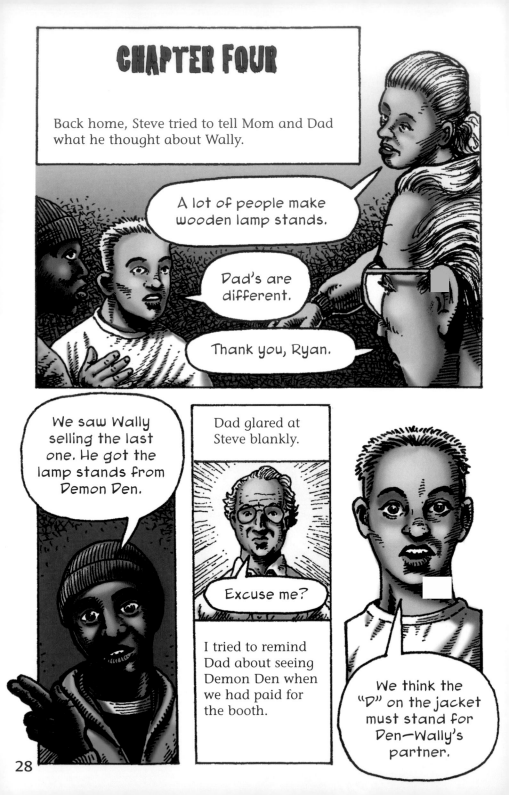

CHAPTER FOUR

Back home, Steve tried to tell Mom and Dad what he thought about Wally.

A lot of people make wooden lamp stands.

Dad's are different.

Thank you, Ryan.

We saw Wally selling the last one. He got the lamp stands from Demon Den.

Dad glared at Steve blankly.

Excuse me?

I tried to remind Dad about seeing Demon Den when we had paid for the booth.

We think the "D" on the jacket must stand for Den—Wally's partner.

That doesn't mean he stole my lamp stands.

Demon and Wally are in it together. They're trying to keep you out of the market.

And why would Wally risk being caught by selling my stuff at the market?

That's jumping to conclusions.

Because he's stupid!

You boys should stop playing detective and go back to playing *Guard Dog*. Stop wasting my time.

Thanks, Dad.

There was no way I was going to tell him that we'd already called the police.

Three days later, Wally turned up at our house. He told us he'd got our address from the market office.

Have you been trying to frame me? Sending your son to snoop and telling tales to the cops?

I have no idea what you're talking about.

I peered around from behind Dad.

I thought you were selling my dad's stuff.

You only saw one lamp stand and that was half wrapped. You're a troublemaker, kid!

Ryan, I told you to stop playing detective.

That did it. As soon as Wally left, Mom was yelling at me.

After that, I decided to stay out of everyone's way.

When I got home from school the next day, Dad was busy carrying cardboard boxes out of his shed.

What risk, Dad? Don't you trust me?

This isn't a game you know, Ryan.

Dad treated me like a child. I was feeling really down, so I went upstairs and played a quick game of *Guard Dog*. I beat my high score by 15, but what did that prove? Soon, Mom would be home, and she'd be yelling at me to finish my history project.

BLEEP BLEEP BLEEP

Suddenly, I heard someone walking up the driveway. I went and looked out of the window, expecting to see Mom or Dad. Instead, I saw a dark figure peering into our car. The studs on his jacket gleamed under the street lamp.

Demon Den!

I rushed downstairs.

CHAPTER FIVE

I should have gone and told Dad, but he was in the shed. There wasn't time to warn him. Instead I grabbed the camcorder, headed outside, and hoped that this risk was worth taking.

I didn't want Demon to see me, so I hurried through the back door and out the alleyway. By the time I got to the street, Demon was already walking away.

I trailed him for a few blocks until he stopped at a phone booth. I waited, wanting to film him, but there was no light in the booth. Fortunately, I could hear him all right, as he spit words into the phone.

Okay, so you're telling me I should have trashed the car last time? So this time I will.

It's me who's taking the risk. Why should you be worried?

No way!

He slammed the phone down and stormed out of the booth.

He walked right by without seeing me, back the way he had come from.

I waited, wanting to let him get a few steps ahead. Before I could follow him, the phone in the booth started ringing.

Demon kept on walking. After a few moments, I picked up the phone and said nothing.

RING RING

Demon? That you? I'll see you at Stoker's hotel in a few minutes like we planned. We'll talk about it, okay?

I looked down the street again, but Demon had turned the corner. I put the phone down and chased after him. When I got to our street, he was gone. I'd lost him, so I went to tell Steve what had happened.

CHAPTER SIX

When we got to Stoker's, Demon's black pick-up truck was outside with two tires on the curb.

It's empty. Let's get in back.

Why?

That way we won't lose them this time.

I didn't like the idea, but as Steve climbed over the tailgate, the door swung open.

Quick!

I had no choice. I scrambled into the back with Steve.

Just keep your head down.

As we ducked out of sight, someone climbed into the pick-up's cab and slammed the door.

Suddenly, the engine roared, and the pick-up lurched forward. As the tires bumped off the curb, we got shaken and rolled all over the cold metal floor. Luckily, the journey was short.

The truck turned down a dark back street and came to a stop. Once the man jumped out, I risked a look over the side.

The pick-up had stopped outside a garage, but I still couldn't see the man's face. He unlocked the garage door. It slowly rattled open. Then the man drove the truck inside, turned off the headlights, got out, and walked off into the dark.

A door slammed at the back of the garage.

I'm sure that wasn't Wally.

He's gone to see someone else. Listen. Can't you hear them?

I heard someone shout: "Where's that darn dog?" Then a shrill squeaking noise as the steel door behind us started rolling down. Steve jumped out of the truck.

SCREEE

Better get out while we can.

We haven't found out who they are yet.

I don't like it here.

Me neither.

The door clanged onto the concrete floor.

45

There was no turning back. We crept along the side wall to a tall stack of cardboard boxes. Through the window of a small room, we could see two men talking—the truck driver and a small man with a moustache.

48

Come on, Ryan! We need to hide.

Steve pulled me back behind the cardboard boxes just as the office door opened. We reached the truck and scrambled into the back before the men appeared.

They unlocked a small metal door built into the big garage door and stepped out into the street.

The door banged shut behind them, and the key turned again. A minute later, a car started up outside. We listened to them drive away.

CHAPTER SEVEN

It was still early evening. It was too soon for Mom and Dad to worry where I might have gone, and go looking for me. Steve said his parents wouldn't be home until eight. By then, Demon Den might steal our car again. Even if Dad was waiting, he wouldn't have the camcorder to record the evidence. We needed to call for help.

OFFICE

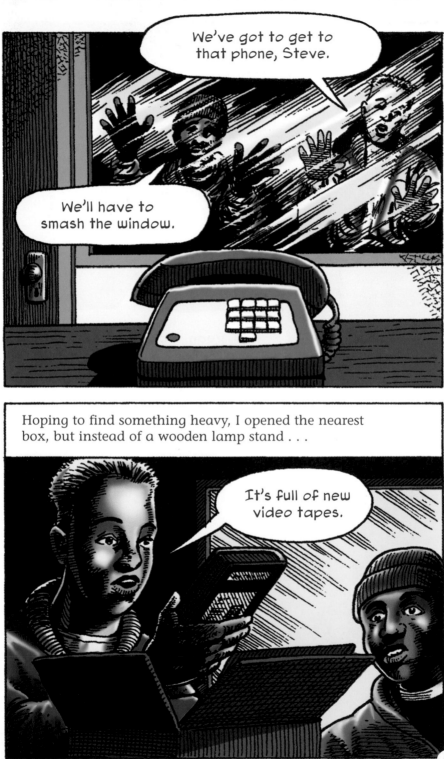

We ripped open more and more boxes. Every one was packed with identical video tapes.

Hey, Ryan, look over there.

Steve discovered a narrow space between the two stacks.

Where's that go?

52

The space had been left as a passage. Through the narrow opening there was a low archway, which led into a hidden room.

The room was dimly lit and filled with stacks of cardboard boxes. The far end of the room glowed with tiny red lights. There were 20 video players, all recording something. There was also a big TV and a video player on a stand.

The TV screen was blank, but the video seemed to be playing.
Steve pressed the eject button.

I suddenly had an idea. Taking the tape from the camcorder, I plugged it into the player. I pressed rewind, then play, and switched on the TV.

The recording I made of the men in the office was loud and clear.

Dog's dangerous. You should ditch him.

I keep him for guarding this place.

We knew the dog wasn't here now. Where was he? I suddenly wondered.

He'd rip them to pieces. That's their fault.

The voices went on.

If the car's trashed, what if the owner comes out?

My finger slipped off the button. The screen went fuzzy and blank.

I had another idea. Demon D must have stolen Dad's car. Wally had sold Dad's lamp stands, but he might have bought them without knowing where they had come from. If so, we must have got it wrong about the "D" standing for Den. Demon D wasn't Wally's partner.

After searching through my pockets, I brought out Wally's card.

I'm going to call Wally.

What for?

CHAPTER EIGHT

But instead of a dog, Demon D burst out of the darkness.

GGGG

GGRR

GRRR

Demon was growling, baring his teeth just like a—

61

Both of us raced through the doorway, trying to dodge him like the dog in *Guard Dog*. But then Demon jumped to the right, blocking our only escape route.

Demon was too quick though. He scrambled up the boxes, snatched hold of my ankle, and started to pull me down.

I tried to run, but his grip was too tight. I kept struggling but couldn't slip free. Then, suddenly . . .

Run!

YAAAHG!

He fell into the TV stand, knocking the video player and switching it on.

With Demon down, Steve and I bolted back through the passageway, across the garage, and to the exit door. Then, I remembered—the only way out would be locked.

As Demon started to get up, Steve fumbled
with the exit lock. It was no use.

We ducked behind the pick-up, but there was nowhere to
hide. I thought we were finished. Demon would get us for
sure. Then, he'd go trash Dad's car and maybe beat up
Dad too. Then I'd have ruined everything.
But weirdly, Demon
ignored us. He walked
straight to the door,
pushed a key into the
lock, and stumbled
out into the street.

We followed him through the door, but he had disappeared.

I bet he's gone to your house.

Steve and I ran all the way to Main Street. In the distance, we could see blue and red lights flashing near my driveway. A police van was outside my house!

This man was shining his flashlight into my car!

What proof?

If you'll all stop yelling at each other, we'll tell you.

Yeah, we'll show you what we discovered.

Hold on, let's get something clear first. Did you call the police?

No. It was probably Wally.

It wasn't me.

Then who?

To find out, we all piled into the police van and made our way back to the garage. The door was still open. As we edged around the boxes and through the hidden passageway, the room seemed dangerously quiet.

Demon might have come back. He's dangerous.

The police were more concerned with all the video recorders and what was playing on the TV screen. I had left my video in there!

So, how do we ditch the dog?

A quick phone call.

Who to?

It's my duty to warn the police that there's a madman about to trash someone's car. Then they can catch Dog red-handed. He's bound to fight back, and he'll get five years in jail for that.

So that's where the call came from.

Before Wally could say more, Dad apologized and asked Wally to supper. I had to wait to get the full story.

My partner, Den, was a great craftsman. He made wonderful stuff. He also took his time and wouldn't be pushed. But working six markets a week, you need a big supply. I had to buy from someone else.

That's why I bought Demon's stuff, which turned out to be your dad's lamp stands. When Den found out about my deal with Demon, he went crazy. We got into a huge argument.

ABOUT THE AUTHOR

Philip Wooderson has written more than 25 books for young people including several stories about a boy named Arf, published by Stone Arch Books.

Philip is married and has one son and one very furry cat. The family divides their time between the coastal town of Ramsgate, England, and the village of Lucignana, in the mountains of Italy.

He enjoys visiting schools and teaching writing. He also likes reading, cooking, gardening, and growing his own food.

GLOSSARY

accuse (uh-KYOOZ)—to claim that someone has done something wrong or illegal

banned (BAND)—to be stopped from doing something or going somewhere

booth (BOOTH)—a stall or stand where someone shows and sells a product

clever (KLEV-ur)—smart and carefully planned

dodging (DOJ-ing)—moving away quickly to avoid something

grimy (GRY-mee)—covered with dirt

hot-wire (HOT-wyr)—to start an automobile illegally without using a key

jumping to conclusions (JUHMP-ing TOO kuhn-KLOO-shunz)—making a decision without having all of the evidence

market (MAR-kit)—a place where many sellers gather for people to buy their goods

shrill (SHRIL)—a high-pitched sound or scream

video pirates (VID-ee-oh PYE-ritz)—people who make illegal copies of videos or DVDs

DISCUSSION QUESTIONS

1. In the story, Ryan decides to take a risk and tries to capture Demon D on his own. Do you think this risk was a good or bad decision? What would you have done? Explain your answers.

2. In chapter four, Ryan tells his parents that he thinks Wally stole the supplies. What evidence does he have to support this guess? Based on this evidence, do you think Ryan was "jumping to conclusions?"

3. Do you think Ryan could have solved the case without his best friend, Steve? List some of the ways Steve helped.

4. Do you think playing *Guard Dog* helped Ryan solve the crime? What useful skills could he have learned from playing a video game? Have you gained any skills from computer or video games? Explain your answers.

WRITING PROMPTS

1. Ryan's friend Steve helped solve the case of the missing supplies. How have your friends helped you in the past? Pick one or two of your best friends, and write a story about how they helped you.

2. What's your favorite video game, movie, or TV show? Imagine you could jump inside your TV or video game and become the main character. Describe your adventures.

3. Demon Dog's boss nicknamed him "Demon Dog." Have you ever had a nickname? If so, write about how you got the new name and if you like it. If you don't have a nickname, make one up and describe your choice.

ALSO PUBLISHED BY STONE ARCH BOOKS

The Haunting of Julia
by Mary Hooper

Before Julia can blow out her birthday candles, the flames vanish into smoke! When she watches a replay on her dad's videotape, she sees a mysterious figure standing behind her shoulder. Julia suspects a ghost has blown out the candles and has come to haunt her.

Lost
by Chris Kreie

Every summer, Eric and his Dad head to the Boundary Waters Canoe Area in northern Minnesota. This year, Eric brought his friend Cris, and the boys want to explore the wilderness on their own. Shortly into the trip, Cris is injured, and Eric must save his friend.

Detective Files
by Steve Bowkett

Someone has stolen a priceless diamond from the city's museum! When police can't catch the crook, they call the world's most famous TV detective — Roy Kane.

Abracadabra
by Alex Gutteridge

Tom is about to come face-to-face with Charlotte, Becca's double. But there's something strange about this, because Charlotte died three hundred and fifty years ago.

STONE ARCH BOOKS,
151 Good Counsel Hill Drive, Mankato, MN 56001
1-800-421-7731
www.stonearchbooks.com

INTERNET SITES

Do you want to know more about subjects related to this book? Or are you interested in learning about other topics? Then check out FactHound, a fun, easy way to find Internet sites.

Our investigative staff has already sniffed out great sites for you!

Here's how to use FactHound:

1. Visit *www.facthound.com*

2. Select your grade level.

3. To learn more about subjects related to this book, type in the book's ISBN number: **1598898299.**

4. Click the **Fetch It** button.

FactHound will fetch the best Internet sites for you.